LOSING IT

LOSING IT

Lesley Glaister

BBC
LARGE
PRINT

First published in 2007 by
Sandstone Press
This Large Print edition published
2009 by BBC Audiobooks
by arrangement with
Sandstone Press

ISBN 978 1 405 62245 5

British Library Cataloguing in Publication Data available

Printed and bound in Great Britain by
CPI Antony Rowe, Chippenham, Wiltshire

Dedicated to the Reader

CHAPTER ONE

It's the day Marion has been dreading. Her friend, Pat, from next door, is moving out. The removal van is there all day on Saturday and Marion helps Pat clean up after the men. She invites Pat round for tea before she leaves and gives her a tin of home-made biscuits to take with her.

After tea, David loads Pat's last few things into her car.

'I'll miss you like mad,' Marion says, giving Pat a hug.

'We'll keep in touch,' Pat says. 'And the lass who's moving in seems very nice.'

'Safe journey,' David says, holding the driver's door open for her.

Marion and David stand by the kerb and wave as Pat drives away. As the car disappears round the corner, tears come into Marion's eyes.

'Cheer up,' David says, but Marion can't help feeling sad. Pat was a good friend and a perfect next-door neighbour. She took in parcels and fed the cat when they went away. She was quiet and friendly and never complained or interfered. On Saturday mornings Marion and Pat always had coffee together. She was a good person to talk to.

A few days later, while Marion and David are eating breakfast, they hear another van arrive. David gets up and looks out of the window.

'The new next-door neighbour,' he says.

Marion gets up to look. She can only see the men carrying furniture. One of them carries a box of bright plastic toys.

'She must have a child,' Marion says.

David turns away. 'More toast?' he asks.

'Do you think I should bake her a cake or something?' Marion says. 'Or

2

no, I won't have time. I'll get a bottle of wine.'

By the time they get home from work, the van has gone. David begins to cook his special pasta with pepperoni and chilli while Marion goes round to say hello to their new neighbour.

A little dark-haired boy opens the door.

'Is your mummy in?' Marion asks.

'Mum,' he yells, 'it's a lady.'

A tall young woman comes to the door. 'Hi,' she says, eyeing the wine bottle.

'Hi,' Marion says. 'I'm Marion from next door. Welcome to the street. David and I live there.' She points.

'I'm Jo,' the woman says. She's skinny with bright brown eyes and short red hair. 'And this is Luke.'

'I'm eight,' he says proudly. 'Do you have any kids?'

'No,' Marion says, 'but we do have a lovely cat. He's called Tigger. Do you like cats?'

'I like all animals,' he says.

'Well you must come round and meet him.'

'Now?'

'Well . . .' Marion hesitates.

'Shut up Luke,' Jo says. 'I'm sure Marion has better things to do.'

'No, it's OK,' Marion says. 'Why not come round? In fact, why not come and eat with us?'

'Are you sure?' Jo says. 'I was about to phone for pizza.'

'We can do an extra bit of pasta. Do you like pasta?' Marion asks Luke.

'It's my second favourite food,' he says.

'What's your first favourite?'

'Pizza,' he says.

Marion laughs.

'Well, at least I've got a bottle of wine to bring!' Jo grins and holds up the bottle.

*　　　*　　　*

4

'Look who's here!' Marion says, as they go through the back door into the kitchen. David is slicing sausage while the pasta bubbles on the stove.

'This is Jo and this is Luke,' she says, 'and this is my husband, David. I thought they could eat with us, David. Can you stretch it?'

'Hi there,' says Jo. 'Hope you don't mind?'

'No, that's fine.' David stares at her for a minute. 'Good to meet you.'

He wipes his hands on a tea-towel before shaking hands first with Jo and then with Luke.

'Where's the cat?' Luke says.

'See if you can find him,' Marion says and Luke runs off to look.

'Sorry I'm such a mess!' Jo says. She's wearing dirty jeans and a T-shirt with a rip under one arm.

'Don't be silly,' Marion says, 'it would be a strange person who moved house in their best clothes.'

5

'How's it going?' David says. He tips more pasta in a pan.

'OK,' Jo says. 'I think!'

'It's meant to be the second—or is it the third?—most stressful thing you can do, moving house,' Marion says. 'Nearly as bad as divorce.'

Jo looks down.

'Oh God, sorry,' Marion says.

But Jo shakes her head. 'It's OK,' she says. 'I took the bastard for every penny he was worth!' and she laughs. Then she sees Marion's face and stops. 'Only joking!'.

'But you are divorced?' Marion says.

'Sort of. Anyway, this is a new start for me.'

David opens the wine and pours three glasses.

'Here's to a new start,' he says. He holds up his glass.

'Cheers,' Jo says.

'A new start,' Marion says.

'Look Mum!' Luke comes back into the room with Tigger in his

6

arms.

'You'll never get rid of him now!' Jo giggles and takes a swig of wine.

CHAPTER TWO

Jo stays so late that Luke falls asleep on the sofa and David carries him back next door. Seeing David with Luke in his arms gives Marion a pang of sadness. They have been trying for a baby for years. They've had all the tests. There's nothing wrong with either of them. But she cannot get pregnant.

Marion sighs and begins loading the dishwasher. They drank three bottles of wine and she has to get up for work in the morning. What a disgrace! Still, she thinks with a smile, at least we get on OK with our new neighbour. She's certainly very different to Pat!

Early on Saturday morning the

doorbell rings. Marion and David are still in bed listening to the radio and drinking tea.

'Leave it,' David says.

'Maybe it's the postman.' Marion gets up and puts on her dressing gown while David grumbles about having his lie in ruined. Luke is standing at the door. He's still in his pyjamas with bare feet.

'Can I play with Tigger?' he says.

'Come in,' Marion says. She makes him some toast and honey. David comes down to get more tea.

'Where's Mum?' he asks.

'Still asleep,' Luke says. 'She sleeps in at weekends.' He squeaks a rubber mouse at Tigger.

'Lucky Mum,' says David.

Luke tries to pick Tigger up but he meows and runs away.

'Make him play with me,' Luke says.

'You can't make him play,' Marion tells him. 'How about another piece of toast?'

'I like chocolate spread best,' he tells Marion when he leaves.

'I'll get some for next time,' she promises.

Later Jo comes round to borrow some milk.

'Want a coffee?' Marion says.

'I hope Luke didn't wake you up?' Jo sits down.

'He was a bit early,' Marion says, 'but I don't mind.'

'Where's David?' Jo asks.

'He plays footie on Saturday,' Marion says, 'and 5-a-side on Sunday. Or else he's out watching a match at the pub.'

'So you don't see much of him?' Jo says.

'Enough!' Marion says.

Jo laughs. She has a big smile and very white teeth. They drink coffee and chat about the people in the street.

'So you're just divorced?' Marion asks.

Jo looks down and bites her

fingernail. 'I don't like to talk about the past,' she says.

'Sorry,' Marion says. 'Does Luke see much of his dad?'

'I'm working on it,' Jo says. 'Oh, by the way, could you babysit for me tonight? I'm going to a party.'

'Fine,' Marion says. 'We're not going out. You can bring Luke here.'

After Jo has gone, Marion looks in the mirror. Her face is pale and her hair is brown and flat. Compared with Jo she is plain and fat. Pat never made her feel like that.

When David gets home, he says, 'We won! And we're going out to celebrate!'

'I can't go out,' Marion says. 'I'm babysitting Luke.'

'But I've booked a restaurant,' he says. 'I thought you'd be pleased.'

'I can't let Jo down,' Marion says.

'Bloody Jo.' David stomps upstairs.

'It'll be fun,' Marion calls after him. 'We can rent a DVD. And make popcorn.'

David stands at the top of the stairs looking down at her. He shrugs his shoulders. 'OK,' he says, 'if that's what you want.'

Jo comes round with Luke at 7 o'clock. She's wearing a silky black dress with a low neckline. Her hair is spiky and her lips are shiny red.

'You look lovely,' Marion says, looking down at her own brown cardigan and furry slippers. I must go on a diet, she thinks.

'Don't know what time I'll be back,' Jo says.

'It doesn't matter. Luke can sleep here,' Marion says. He snuggles under her arm.

'Are you sure? Brilliant!' Jo kisses Luke and leaves a red smudge on his cheek. 'See you tomorrow then,' she says and wobbles off in her high heels.

CHAPTER THREE

Jo does not come back to pick Luke up till Sunday afternoon. It's a sunny spring day, and Marion, David and Luke are out in the garden. David reads the paper while Luke helps Marion put in some pansies.

'I'm so sorry,' Jo says. 'I got in late and then I overslept.'

'It's fine,' Marion says. 'We had fun.'

'We watched a film and made popcorn!' Luke says. 'And Tigger slept on my bed with me.'

'Nice to have a child in the house,' Marion says. 'We'll babysit anytime. Won't we David?'

David looks up from his paper. 'A bit of notice would be nice,' he says, 'in case we want to go out.'

'David!' says Marion.

'No, it's OK,' Jo says, but her voice is a little stiff. 'Come on Luke.' And she goes home.

'You could have been more friendly,' Marion says.

He raises his eyebrows at her.

'Alone at last,' he says.

*   *   *

The next night Jo comes round just as Marion and David are about to go to bed.

'Can you help me?' she says.

'What's wrong?' Marion asks.

'Can't it wait?' David says, looking at his watch. 'It's late.'

'No, it's OK,' Marion says. 'What is it?'

'There's a great big spider in my bath,' she says, 'and I'm petrified of spiders.'

'Me too,' says Marion. 'David?'

David sighs. 'Women!' he says. 'Come on then.' And he goes next door with Jo.

Marion puts on her nightie and gets into bed, waiting for David to

13

come back. He's a long time, much longer than it would take to remove a spider from a bath.

When he does come back she says, 'Why were you so long?'

'No sign of the spider,' he says, 'so I had to look for it.'

'Did you find it?'

He shakes his head and takes off his shirt. 'She's going to decorate the whole house,' he says.

'That's a shame,' Marion says. 'Pat only did it all before she left.'

'She thinks it's too old fashioned.'

He gets into bed and thumps his pillow into shape.

'She got me to look at some paint charts,' he says. 'Sorry it took so long.'

*   *   *

On Saturday morning Luke rings the doorbell again while Marion and David are still in bed. 'Bloody pest!' David grumbles as Marion gets up.

14

'Bring me a cuppa will you?'

'Good morning Luke.' Marion opens the door. He's in his pyjamas again and his feet are bare. 'You should put your slippers on,' she says.

'I don't have slippers,' he says.

Marion finds him a big pair of socks to warm his feet up. 'Now, shall we make some pancakes?' she says.

'Yay!' he says. 'Yum yum!'

Marion shows him how to beat the eggs into the flour and milk. They eat the pancakes with lemon and sugar.

Luke licks the sugar off his fingers. 'That was cool,' he says. 'Mum never makes pancakes.'

Later Jo comes round. Her make up is smudged all round her eyes. 'Late night,' she says and yawns.

'Coffee?' Marion says.

'Mum, we made pancakes,' Luke says.

'Ta.' Jo smiles at Marion. 'You're a

star. Can you have Luke again tonight?'

'I can't,' Marion says. 'Sorry. David and I are going to a party.'

'Oh.' Jo chews her fingernail and frowns. 'No problem,' she says. 'I'll just have to stay in then.'

'Can't you ask someone else?'

Jo shakes her head. 'Everyone goes out on Saturdays,' she complains.

'Even us this week!' Marion says. 'I'm sorry. Any other time.'

At 7 o'clock Marion puts on her black trousers, her green velvet top and her high heeled sandals. She sprays herself with perfume and puts on lipstick and mascara. David wears a new white shirt. His face is smooth and he smells of aftershave.

'You look beautiful,' he says and kisses her.

'You're not so bad yourself!' she says.

As David picks up his car keys, the doorbell rings. Jo is on the doorstep and she's crying.

'Come in,' Marion says. 'What on earth's the matter?'

'I just had a phone call from a friend,' she says. 'Her husband's got cancer and she's in a right state. She wants me to go round—'

'And you want us to have Luke?' David says. 'But we're off to a party.'

'I know it's a lot to ask,' Jo says.

'Can't you take him with you?' Marion says.

Jo sniffs and shakes her head. Her eyelashes are all wet and spiky. 'See, he's allergic to her parrot.'

'Her parrot?' David says.

'I thought he loved animals?' Marion says.

'He's allergic to feathers.'

Marion looks at David.

He shrugs his shoulders. 'OK, OK,' he says, but he looks angry.

Jo's face lights up in a brilliant smile. 'Thank you!' she says. She kisses David on his cheek and hugs Marion. 'You're both stars!' She goes

17

home to fetch Luke. Marion wipes off her lipstick. She takes off her sandals and puts on her furry slippers.

'We could get a takeaway?' she says.

'Mind if I go?' David says.

Marion thinks about it. It's his mate Ken's divorce party and he promised to be there.

'OK,' she says. 'Say hi to Ken for me. I wish I was coming.'

'You should have said no to Jo then,' he says.

Luke comes round with his pyjamas and toothbrush.

'Mum says I'm staying the night,' he says. He gives Marion his stuff and runs upstairs to find Tigger. She looks out of the window and sees Jo getting into a taxi. She's wearing fishnet tights and a short black skirt. She waves when she sees Marion looking and jumps into the taxi. Marion watches it drive away. She puts the TV on and opens a can of beans.

CHAPTER FOUR

'How was your friend?' Marion asks Jo when she comes round for Luke on Sunday afternoon. It's raining. David's out watching the football in the pub.

'Which friend?' Jo says.

Marion puts teabags into two mugs.

'The one whose husband has got cancer?' she says.

Jo's hand flies to her mouth. 'Oh,' she says. 'Sue? She's gutted. I took her out for a drink.'

'What kind of cancer is it?'

'Something down there,' Jo says. 'His balls.'

'Testicular?'

Jo nods.

'Ouch,' Marion says.

'She's gutted they won't be able to

have kids,' Jo says, 'even if he gets better.'

Marion sips her tea. She pushes a plate of biscuits towards Jo.

'Luke helped me make these,' she says. 'They look funny but they taste good.'

'No ta,' Jo says. 'I'm watching my weight.'

'But you're so skinny,' Marion says. 'I wish I was that thin.' She puts her own biscuit back on the plate.

Jo smiles. 'Do you and David plan on having kids?'

'We'd love to,' Marion says. 'We've been trying for years.'

Jo pats her on the hand. 'Poor you,' she says, 'and there's me getting pregnant at the first pop! Not fair is it?'

Marion shakes her head.

'Does David mind much?' Jo asked.

'Yes. He'd love a kid,' Marion says. 'And so would I.'

'You can always borrow Luke.' Jo

laughs. 'He gets on my nerves, me all on my own with him.'

'But he's sweet,' Marion says. 'Where's his dad?'

'Good question,' Jo says. 'Thanks for the tea. And thanks for having him.' She gets up. 'Luke,' she calls. 'We're going.'

'Can I watch the end of the film?' Luke shouts from the other room.

'Do you mind?' Jo asks.

'Of course not,' Marion says.

*   *   *

The next Saturday Jo asks David to give her a lift to B&Q to get some paint.

'I would get it delivered,' she says, 'only I want to make a start today.'

'We'll have to be quick,' David says. 'The match starts at 12.'

Luke goes in the car with them. Marion feels lonely. She washes the kitchen floor and does the ironing and then she goes out shopping. By the time she gets back, David has gone to the match. Luke is sitting on the doorstep.

'Mum made me go out,' he says, 'so I don't get paint on me.'

'Come in then.' Marion is glad to see him. She gives him a bag of crisps and he sits on the sofa with Tigger on his knee.

'I wish I lived with you,' he says.

'You're only next door,' Marion says.

She goes into the kitchen to start cooking. They have friends coming round that night. She makes a beef casserole and a cheesecake. Luke helps her bash up the biscuits for the cheesecake base.

David gets home at 4 o'clock. He's happy because his team won. He picks Marion up and twirls her round. He smells of beer.

'Fancy a quickie?' he says.

'But Luke's here,' Marion says. 'Make it a cup of tea instead?'

He groans and goes upstairs to

change.

*   *   *

Their friends Jean and Ron come round at 7 o'clock. David opens a bottle of red wine and they all stand outside in the sunshine waiting for the potatoes to cook. Jo comes into the garden. She's wearing paint-splashed jeans and a T-shirt that shows her flat brown tummy.

'Oh sorry,' she says. 'I didn't know you had company. I was going to borrow David.'

'Not now,' David says.

'Oh aye,' says Ron, 'what's this?' He waggles his eyebrows at David.

'Don't be daft,' says Jean.

'Just to help me with a tricky bit of ceiling,' Jo says.

'Time for a glass of wine?' Marion says.

'No. Oh go on then,' Jo replies.

'Where's Luke?' Marion asks.

'I'll get him.'

23

Jo goes next door and comes back with her lipstick on, just as the potatoes are done. Tigger's in the garden and Luke goes to play with him.

'We're just about to eat,' David says, frowning at her.

'Oh sorry,' Jo says.

'Do you want to join us?' Marion says. She crosses her fingers, hoping Jo will say no.

But 'Go on, then,' is what she says.

CHAPTER FIVE

The doorbell rings. It's late on Sunday morning and Marion and David are still in bed. The sun shines through the curtains. They are both hung over. Jo, Ron and Jean did not leave till 3 a.m.

David groans. 'Don't go,' he says.

'But it will be Luke,' Marion says.

'Can't Jo look after him?'

'She'll be asleep,' Marion says. She starts to get up. David grabs hold of her arm.

'Don't go,' he says again.

Marion pulls away. 'I can't leave him on the doorstep.'

She goes downstairs to let Luke in.

'I've got a present for you,' she says. She gives Luke a box. He takes out a pair of Spider Man slippers.

'Cool!' he says. He puts them on and jumps around pretending to be Spider Man.

She takes David up a cup of tea but he's in a sulk. She does all the washing up and puts the bottles out. Then she takes Luke to the shop to buy milk and the Sunday papers. He won't take the slippers off. She buys him a comic and a Curly Wurly.

In the afternoon Jo comes round. She has a cup of tea with Marion. David's back from 5-a-side and reading the paper in the garden. It's hot. Jo's wearing tiny cut-off jeans. She has long smooth legs. She stands in front of David in his deck chair.

'Could you help me with the ceiling?' she asks.

Marion sees David look at Jo's legs. He can't help it, she's standing right in front of him. There's nowhere else to look.

'Please?' Jo says. 'It won't take long.'

David looks at Marion. 'Go on,' Marion says. 'I'll take Luke to the park.'

'You're a star,' says Jo.

Marion and Luke drive to the park. She watches him on the swing and the roundabout. She buys him an ice lolly and they sit on a bench in the sunshine feeding bread to the ducks.

When they get home, David isn't back. Luke plays with Tigger and watches a cartoon on TV.

At 5 o'clock Marion takes Luke home. The back door is open and Luke races straight in.

'Hello?' Marion calls up the stairs.

She can hear them laughing.

'Hi there,' Jo calls. 'Come up.'

Marion thinks it's sad that Jo has painted all over Pat's wallpaper. But it does look more modern. David is sitting on a ladder in the bedroom. The ceiling is finished and he's drinking a can of beer.

'What do you think?' Jo says.

'Nice,' says Marion. The walls are pale yellow and the ceiling white. It looks bright and sunny.

'We could do our room like this,' David says.

Marion nods but really she likes their bedroom just the way it is.

'David's going to help me with the stairs next week,' Jo says. She swigs her beer. 'Oh, do you want a drink?'

'No thanks,' Marion says. 'Are you coming home now David?'

He finishes his can and jumps down off the ladder.

'You don't mind David helping me, do you Marion?' Jo says.

'Of course not,' Marion says.

*　　*　　*

'What's up?' David asks Marion later. It's bedtime. She's been quiet all evening.

'I don't know,' she says.

'Is it because I'm helping Jo to decorate?'

'Maybe.' Marion shrugs.

David laughs. 'For God's sake!' he says. 'First you tell me off for being unfriendly, now you don't want me to help her.'

'It's not that,' Marion says.

'What then?'

'I've been wanting the kitchen done for years,' she says.

David sighs.

'Do you like her?' Marion asks in a small voice.

'I think she's a pain in the neck,' David says.

'Good,' says Marion. 'I think so too.'

CHAPTER SIX

David is over at Jo's every night that week. And every night, Marion babysits Luke and cooks tea for everyone. David and Jo come in all painty and giggly, eat their tea and then go back while Marion washes up and Luke watches TV.

On Friday the hall and stairs are finished. Marion goes round to see. The walls are sky blue and the woodwork is white.

'It looks lovely,' Marion says.

Jo pours them all a glass of wine.

'I'm doing Luke's room next,' she says.

'I chose the paint myself,' Luke says. 'It's red.'

'It might look awful,' Jo says, 'but I said he could choose.'

'Red is my favourite colour,' Luke says. 'Like a fire engine.'

'I thought maybe just one wall

29

red,' Jo says.

'It's a shame David can't help you,' Marion says, 'but we're starting on the kitchen next week.'

David looks startled. 'Are we?' he says.

'While you're in the mood,' Marion says.

'Fine,' Jo says. She gives David a look. 'I can wait.'

Jo orders a Chinese takeaway as a thank you. They sit in her kitchen and eat chop suey, chow mein and crispy pancake rolls. They drink too much wine again.

'Do you want to come shopping with me tomorrow?' Marion says to Jo. 'We could have a girly lunch.'

'But who would look after Luke?' Jo says. Then she blushes. 'Sorry. Did that sound bad?'

'David could mind Luke, couldn't you David?' Marion says.

'Suppose so.'

'That's settled then,' says Marion.

＊　　　＊　　　＊

Marion and Jo take the bus into town. They choose new curtains for Marion's kitchen. Jo buys a short white dress in a sale. Marion picks up brochures from a travel agent. They go into a wine bar for lunch and have pasta and big glasses of white wine.

'You're such a good pal,' Jo says. 'And Luke loves you.'

Marion smiles. 'It's nice to have you both living next door,' she says.

'It's hard being on my own,' Jo says. 'I hope you don't mind me borrowing David sometimes?'

'Of course not,' Marion says.

They look at the brochures.

'I'd choose Spain,' Jo says.

'I'd love to go to Greece,' Marion says, 'but David's scared of flying.'

'David's scared of flying!' Jo laughs. 'I never knew that!'

'Why should you?' Marion said.

'No reason,' Jo said. She sips her

wine and flicks through the brochure.

'Where do you come from?' Marion asks.

'Bridge Town,' Jo says.

'That's funny,' Marion says. 'That's where David's from.'

'Well, it's a big place,' Jo says. 'Another glass of wine?'

When they get home Jo comes in for a cup of tea. David and Luke are playing with David's old Subbuteo game on the kitchen table.

'Goal!' shouts David, as they come in. 'Hi girls, have fun?'

'It was lovely,' Marion says. 'You?'

'It's brilliant!' Luke says. 'This is a cool game, Mum.'

'It's nice for Luke to have a bit of male company,' Jo says and giggles. 'You can be his role model, David!'

'These are the curtains,' Marion says, getting them out to show. 'And I got paint charts too.'

'And I got this in a sale.' Jo gets her tiny dress out of a bag and holds it up against her.

'Did you get me anything?' Luke says.

'What about this?' Marion says, bringing a chocolate bar out of her bag.

'Such a shame you can't have kids of your own,' Jo says.

There is a silence.

'Why can't you have kids?' Luke asks.

'It's not that we can't,' David says. He looks angry.

'Maybe we'd better go,' Jo says. 'Come on Luke.'

'She really is a pain in the neck,' David says when they've gone. Angrily, he packs the Subbuteo back in its box.

'She's not that bad,' Marion says. 'It's hard for her on her own.' She gives him a mug of tea. 'I'm glad you had fun with Luke,' she says.

'I'll watch the match now.' David takes his tea into the other room. Marion follows him.

'It still might happen,' she says. 'There's nothing wrong with us.'

David smiles. He puts his tea down and looks at the clock. 'It's twenty minutes till kick off,' he says. 'Want to give it another try?'

CHAPTER SEVEN

Marion and David decorate the kitchen together. It's fun. They listen to loud music as they work, and eat fish suppers in the garden. David puts new tiles round the cooker and buys fresh lino for the floor. It's hot enough to leave the door and windows open and the paint dries quickly.

When it's finished Jo comes round to see. She brings Marion a bunch of flowers she's picked from Pat's garden. Of course it's Jo's garden now, but to Marion it's still Pat's. Pat put in all the plants and shrubs and spent hours out there watering and weeding.

Marion has baked a cake and they drink sparkling wine. There's lemonade for Luke, who has his own special glass in the cupboard now. Marion and David are off on holiday on Friday. Marion gives Jo the key. Luke is going to feed Tigger and Jo will keep an eye on the place.

'The kitchen's lovely,' Jo says, looking round.

The evening sun shines on the new tiles and the fresh white paint round the windows.

'It is, isn't it?' Marion says.

'Have you any of this green paint left over?' Jo asks. 'I could use it in my toilet.'

'A bit,' says Marion.

'But we're keeping it for touch-ups,' David says.

Marion shows Luke some pictures of Cornwall. 'We're going to Tintagel,' she tells him. 'It's where King Arthur lived. Do you know about King Arthur?'

Luke shakes his head.

'I'll bring you back a book about him,' Marion promises.

'You're so lucky,' Jo says. She holds out her glass for some more wine. She gives Luke a hard look and nudges him.

'What?' he says. Then, 'Oh. I wish we could come with you.'

'Luke!' Jo says. 'Really! Marion and David don't want us with them.'

'Well . . .' begins Marion.

'No,' David says. 'Sorry. It wouldn't work.'

Jo shrugs. 'Oh well,' she says. 'We'll look after the house while you're away.'

'Tigger will be like my own cat!' Luke says, grinning all over his face.

'Have a great holiday,' Jo says, 'and happy birthday for next week, Marion.'

'What's the betting she'll turn up?' David says when she's gone home.

'She wouldn't do that!' Marion

says.

'She'd better not,' said David.

CHAPTER EIGHT

The sun shines and the sea sparkles. The holiday cottage is perched on the edge of the cliff. From the garden they can see far out to sea and smell the salt and seaweed. Every day they go for long walks. Some nights they eat at the pub, and some nights they sit in the garden drinking wine, listening to the waves and watching the seagulls swoop over the cliff.

Marion's birthday is on Friday and they're going home on Saturday. On Thursday night they have cider and Cornish pasties in the pub, then walk home along the cliff top. The sun is setting on the sea and the waves are like fire.

Marion suddenly feels very sad.

'What if we never have a baby?' she says.

David stops. He turns and puts his finger under her chin. 'It doesn't matter,' he says.

'Are you sure?'

'All I need is you,' he says.

It sounds so cheesey that Marion laughs.

'This has been the best holiday ever,' she says.

'Who needs to fly?' David says. 'Who needs Spain? Who needs Greece?'

'And Jo never turned up!' Marion says.

'Don't bring her into it,' David says. He stops and takes an envelope out of his pocket. 'This is for you,' he says.

Marion takes it. 'But it's not my birthday till tomorrow.'

'Open it!' He grins like a little boy.

Marion looks inside the envelope and finds a voucher for a Health Spa. A Beauty Day with a massage, lunch and a facial.

'For tomorrow,' David says.

'Thank you!' Marion throws her arms round him. 'I've always wanted to do that!'

'I can drop you off in the morning,' he says, 'and pick you up later. We'll go to that little fish restaurant in the village.'

'It sounds like a perfect day,' Marion says. 'A perfect end to the holiday.'

*   *   *

When they get back Marion goes into the garden to get their swimming things off the washing line. She stands outside in the fresh sea air. She wishes they could stay for ever. From inside she hears David's mobile ring. With her arms full of towels she goes into the kitchen.

'What?' Marion hears him say. He is turned away from her. His voice sounds shocked. 'When? How? Oh God. I'll tell Marion. I'll ring you back.'

'What's up?' Marion says. She drops the towels on the table.

'That was Jo,' David says.

Marion's heart sinks. 'What's happened?'

'We've been burgled.'

Marion puts her hand over her mouth. 'Oh my God,' she says.

'She doesn't know what to do,' David says. 'The police need to know what's missing.'

'We'll have to go straight home,' Marion says.

'I don't know,' David says. 'Trust Jo to ruin things.'

'It's not her fault!' says Marion.

'How did the burglars get in?' David says. 'Maybe she left the door unlocked.'

'I wonder what they've taken,' Marion says. 'I hope Tigger's all right.'

'They wouldn't steal the cat!'

'Cats do get stolen,' Marion points out.

David goes out in the garden and walks up and down, thinking about what to do. Marion starts packing her clothes.

David comes back in. 'No,' he says. 'Stop. I don't want you to miss your Beauty Day.'

'But we have to go. We can't leave Jo to sort it on her own.'

'I'll go,' he says. 'You can have your day, stay the night in a B&B, then get the train back.'

'But it'll cost a fortune!' Marion says.

'I don't care,' David says. 'I'm not having your birthday ruined.'

'But how could I relax?'

'You will,' he says, 'and I want you to have your birthday treat. I want you to be pampered.'

David rings Jo. 'I'm coming back,' he says. He packs the car and sets off to drive north right through the night.

41

CHAPTER NINE

In the morning Marion takes a taxi to the Health Spa. She feels like a film star as the taxi carries her up the long tree-lined drive. The building is old and beautiful. There's a fountain, peacocks and a lake with carp.

A receptionist in uniform opens her taxi door and greets Marion. He shows her round and gives her a lunch menu and a fluffy white robe to wear. She books herself a massage for before lunch and a facial for afterwards. She swims in the huge blue pool. She lies on the massage table feeling the warm oily hands of the masseur on her body. She eats a crab salad for her lunch, but she doesn't enjoy it. She feels sick. She's worried about the burglary and what's been taken. She's worried that David might be angry with Jo. She's worried about Jo.

After lunch she gets dressed. She goes to reception. 'I've been called away,' she says. 'Could you get me a taxi to the station please?'

'That's a shame, Madam,' the receptionist says.

She doesn't ring David. He wants her to stay and he might talk her out of leaving. She stands outside in the sunshine waiting for the taxi. It is so peaceful. She can hear the fountain and a peacock squawking in the distance, but they are the only sounds.

The train gets in at midnight. She takes a taxi and it's nearly 1 o'clock when she arrives home. She's exhausted. The light is still on in the kitchen. Instead of going straight in, she stands in the flower bed to look through the kitchen window. She sees David sitting at the table with a glass of wine. And she sees Jo pouring herself a glass. Jo's wearing the tiny white dress. Marion watches Jo's mouth moving but she can't hear what she says. She sees her laughing, and David laughing.

Marion's hand shakes as she opens the door.

'Hello,' she says.

Jo goes white and the smile drops from her face.

David gets up. 'Marion!' he says. 'What are you doing back?'

'I was worried,' Marion says. 'I had to come home.'

She looks around at her new kitchen. The doorframe and window frame are dusted with fingerprint powder. It looks dirty now.

'A glass of wine?' Jo asks.

'No thanks.'

'Maybe I should go,' Jo says.

'Maybe you should,' Marion says. 'Where's Luke?'

'At home in bed,' Jo says. 'I only just popped in.'

One o'clock in the morning is a funny time to be popping in, Marion thinks.

'Oh, happy birthday,' Jo says.

'It was yesterday.' Marion looks at the clock.

'See you later,' Jo says and she goes home.

David hugs Marion. 'You must have cut your Beauty Day short.'

'I left after lunch.'

'But I paid for a whole day. And what about the B&B?'

'How could I stay?'

'Well anyway, I'm glad you're back.'

'Are you?' Marion says.

'Of course I am!'

David tells her about going to the police station and listing everything that had been taken.

'What has been taken?' Marion says.

'It's not too bad,' David says. 'The DVD recorder. My computer. Some CDs. Some of your jewellery but I'm not sure what.'

'Oh my God.'

'We'll get it all on insurance. The police say we got off lightly. Jo disturbed them.'

'Jo disturbed them?'

'She heard a noise and came round.'

'Did she see them?'

'Just the back of someone running. A kid.'

Marion goes upstairs. The lock is broken on her jewellery box and the thief has taken a gold chain, a frog-shaped brooch and a ruby and pearl ring. The ring was her granny's. She won't get that back on insurance. She sits on the bed and cries. She's tired. She feels sick. She hates the feeling that a thief has been in her bedroom. Her underwear is all over the floor and all the drawers hang open.

David comes upstairs. 'Don't cry,' he says. 'I was going to tidy up before you got back.'

'They took my granny's ring,' she says.

'Bastards,' says David. He puts his arm round her.

She sniffs. 'What was Jo doing

here?'

'She saw the light on,' he says.

'So?'

'She couldn't sleep. She's scared the burglars might come back to hers.'

'So? That's not your problem is it?'

'We should be thankful to her,' David says.

'I don't like her being round so late when I'm not here.'

David shrugs. 'Come on,' he says. 'You look shattered. Time for bed.'

CHAPTER TEN

In the morning Luke is round to wake them up. Marion gets out of bed to let him in. She's still half asleep. He gives her a tight hug.

'I'm glad you're back,' he says. 'Mum was cross while you were away.'

47

'I'm glad I'm back too,' she says.
She puts the kettle on.

'You looked after Tigger very well,' she says. 'Thank you.'

Marion gives Luke a stick of rock and a book about King Arthur and the Knights of the Round Table. He sits at the table and sucks the rock while he looks at the pictures.

'Mum was like a hero,' he says. He's all pink round his mouth from the rock.

'Yes,' Marion says. 'I will say thank you to her.'

Later Marion rings the police and describes the jewellery that has been stolen.

'Do you think I'll get it back?' she asks.

'Doubt it, darling,' the police-woman says.

Marion puts on her rubber gloves and scrubs away the fingerprint powder. She puts all her clothes in the washing machine. She rings up and orders a burglar alarm.

'Just been burgled?' asks the man.

'Yes,' she says.

He sighs. 'Shutting the door after the horse has bolted,' he says. 'Everyone does that.'

Jo comes round for Luke.

'We have to go shopping for shoes,' she says. 'School on Monday.'

'I'm glad you disturbed the burglars,' Marion says. 'They would have taken more. Thank you.'

'It's nothing,' Jo says.

'Time for a coffee?'

'Where's David?' Jo says.

'Why?'

'Doesn't matter.'

'He's gone to the garden centre to buy a new fence,' Marion says. 'Do you want a coffee?'

'OK.' Jo sits down.

She's more tanned than Marion, even though Marion's the one who's been on holiday.

'Been on a sunbed?' Marion says.

'No,' Jo says. 'I just tan easily.' She's dyed her hair an even brighter red and is wearing too much lipstick.

Marion puts the coffee on the table. She shuts the door to the other room where Luke's watching TV.

'What were you doing here last night?' she says.

'Nothing.'

'It was late,' Marion says.

'We didn't expect you,' Jo says.

'We?'

There's a long silence.

'We?' Marion says again. Her hands are shaking.

'If you must know, David asked me round,' Jo says.

Marion sits down.

'Why?' she says.

'How should I know?' Jo says.

'He's my husband,' Marion says quietly.

'I know,' Jo says. 'That's what I told him.'

'What?'

'Nothing.' Jo stood up. 'Luke,' she calls. 'Time to go.'

Luke comes through.

'Bye Marion,' he says. He hugs her round her waist. He's all sticky from the rock. 'Can I come back later?'

'We'll see,' Marion says.

*   *   *

David comes back from the garden centre and starts fixing up the new fence. Marion sits on a deck chair and watches him. The sun is hot and he takes his shirt off. He looks brown and fit. When he's finished he drops his hammer on the grass and sits down.

'What's up?' he says.

'Nothing.'

'You're too quiet!' He smiles at her.

Marion doesn't smile back. She takes a deep breath. 'Jo told me you asked her round last night,' she says. She watches his face.

'That's rubbish,' he says. 'Why would I?'

'Why would she lie?'

He shades his eyes against the sun. 'I don't know,' he says.

'What if I hadn't come back?' she says.

'I don't know. Nothing.'

'She was wearing that short dress.'

'I didn't notice what she was wearing.'

'Liar,' Marion says.

David laughs. 'OK,' he says. 'So I did notice the dress. But I didn't ask her round. I just wanted to go to bed. Alone.'

He looks at her for a long time. 'Do you believe me?' he says.

'If I do,' Marion says at last, 'it means Jo is lying.'

David nods.

'But why?'

'She's a lass with problems,' David says.

'What do you mean?'

'Lonely,' he says, 'insecure. But don't you be insecure. There's no need to be.'

'Really?'

'Really.' David gets up from the grass. He bends over to kiss her. He smells of sweat.

'You need a shower,' she says.

David grins, 'Join me?' he says. He pulls her up from the deck chair and into the house.

CHAPTER ELEVEN

Marion feels guilty for doubting David. On Sunday she decides to do his favourite meal—roast chicken with all the trimmings. While it's cooking Luke plays with Tigger. He comes through into the kitchen and sniffs.

'That smells good,' he says. 'Can I stay for tea?'

Marion thinks about it. She hasn't spoken to Jo since yesterday morning and doesn't want to. But it's a big chicken. And it would be good for Luke to have a proper meal. Jo usually gets Luke's tea from the chippie or microwaves a ready meal. It would be good to show David that she trusts him, and to show Jo that she isn't threatened.

And then she has another good idea. David's friend Ken is just divorced. Maybe he'll fancy Jo. And, even better, maybe she'll fancy him.

'OK,' she says to Luke. 'Run along now and ask your mum to come too.'

She phones Ken and invites him.

'That sounds great,' he says. 'I'll be there.'

Marion makes a trifle and puts it in the fridge. She feels nervous. She goes upstairs and changes into a sun dress. She puts make up on. But when she looks in the mirror her heart sinks. She can't begin to compete with Jo. She's five years older for a start and, with all the Cornish pasties and ice creams on holiday, has put on pounds. Her hair is flat and her arms are fat. She takes the dress off and puts on a skirt and a long sleeved shirt. She wipes off the make up. She wishes she hadn't asked Jo or Ken. She wants it to be just her and David, like it always used to be.

Ken turns up early with two bottles of wine.

'What's this in aid of?' he asks.

'Just thought it would be nice to see you,' Marion says.

'You look well,' he says.

Marion thinks she knows what he means by well. He means fat.

David opens the wine. Marion takes the chicken out of the oven. It's huge and crispy and golden.

'Wow,' Ken says. 'Home cooking. You can't beat it.'

Jo comes through the back door. She's wearing the white dress again. Her arms look slim and brown. She's spiked up her hair and smells of perfume.

'Who's this?' she says, surprised to see Ken there.

'This is Ken,' Marion says, 'and

Ken, this is Jo from next door.'

'And I'm Luke,' Luke says, 'and I'm nearly nine.'

'Pleased to meet you, Luke,' Ken says, looking at Jo's legs.

They all drink wine and talk about the football and the hot weather. Marion sits Ken next to Jo at the table. She sees Jo trying to catch David's eye but she sees David ignoring her. Ken looks at her plenty though, from the hem of her short dress to her bright red hair. Jo drinks too much wine and flirts with Ken. Marion relaxes and smiles at David.

'Delicious meal,' he says.

'Too right,' Ken said.

'I've got the wishbone,' Jo says. 'Who wants to pull it with me?'

'I will!' Luke and Ken say together.

'Don't you want to, David?' Jo asks.

He shakes his head.

'Come on Ken,' Jo says. She holds it out to him.

'That's not fair,' Luke says.

Ken and Jo pull the wishbone. Jo gets the big half.

'What did you wish for?' Ken asks.

'That would be telling,' Jo says. She gives David a sly smile.

Both the men ask for more chicken and roast potatoes.

'Leave room for the trifle,' Marion says.

'I love trifle,' Luke says. 'It's my second favourite pudding.'

'I love trifle,' Jo says. She licks her lips and smiles at Ken. 'All that cream.'

Ken goes red in the face.

After the meal Marion shows Ken and Jo their holiday photos.

'There's David in front of our cottage,' she says, 'and there's me in front of our cottage.'

'Don't you have any of you together?' Jo says.

'No, because one of us was always taking the picture,' David says.

'Shame,' Jo says.

Marion makes coffee. Ken sits

next to Jo on the sofa and he tells her about his plumbing business.

'There's something funny about my toilet,' she says, and giggles.

'Want me to come and look?' Ken says.

'Yes,' Jo says. 'How about right now? We can have a night-cap.' She looks at David, but he just gets up and starts clearing the cups away.

'Thanks for the meal,' Ken says.

'No problem,' Marion says. 'I'm glad you came. Any time.'

Jo, Ken and Luke go off next door. Marion shuts the back door and leans against it.

'Problem solved,' she says.

But David frowns. 'I don't want to see Ken messed around,' he says. 'He's not over Susan yet.'

'Jo might not mess him around,' Marion points out. 'They might fall madly in love and live happily after.'

David snorts. 'And elephants might land on Mars,' he says.

CHAPTER TWELVE

Jo and Ken do soon become an item, which means that Marion and David do a lot more babysitting.

One hot Saturday, David takes Luke to the park to play football. Marion goes shopping. On her way home, she decides to stop off at the park to see them. The park is packed and at first she can't find them. The she hears David's voice. They're over by the fence. Marion goes to the Mr Whippy van, buys three ice creams and goes over to surprise them.

'Yey!' Luke says when he sees the ice cream. 'Hi Marion!'

'I thought you might be hot,' Marion says.

David kisses her cheek and takes his. 'Ta for this,' he says. 'We weren't expecting you.'

'No we weren't,' Jo says.

Marion jumps. 'And I didn't expect to see you,' she says. Her melting ice cream drips down her hand. Suddenly she can't eat it.

'I'll have it if you don't want it,' Jo says.

Marion hands it over and watches Jo lick it with her sharp pink tongue.

'I thought you were out with Ken,' she says.

'Later.'

'But I thought that was why we're babysitting today.'

'David likes to spend time with Luke. Don't you David?' Jo says.

But David is talking to Luke and doesn't answer.

'And I like to watch them together,' Jo says. 'No harm in that, is there?'

'I'm getting good,' Luke says. He has a blob of ice cream on his nose. 'Football's my second favourite sport.'

'What's the first?' David asks.

'Sky diving,' Luke says. He

crunches his cone.

David laughs and pats his head.

'See. They get on like a house on fire,' Jo says.

'Come on,' David says, 'let's get back to training.'

Marion stands beside Jo while David and Luke kick about a bit. David teaches Luke to do a header.

'He's a natural!' David shouts to them.

'It's good for Luke to have a man about,' Jo says.

Marion tries to be friendly. 'Yes. And David's good with kids,' she says.

'Shame,' Jo says.

*   *   *

Later Jo does go out with Ken. Marion gives Luke his tea in front of the TV while she and David have an Indian takeaway in the kitchen. Marion is just plucking up courage to ask David how often Jo has joined him in the park with Luke, when the door opens and Jo walks in.

Marion waits for Ken to appear behind her, but he doesn't. 'Where's Ken?' she asks.

'It's over.' Jo sits down and helps herself to a glass of wine.

'Why?' Marion says.

'Don't know.' Jo shrugs. She picks a bit of popadom off David's plate and dips it into the chutney. 'He just didn't do it for me,' she says.

Marion sighs. 'Plenty more fish in the sea,' she says.

Jo giggles. 'Yes, but I don't want a fish, do I?' She looks at David.

He frowns. 'Have you come to fetch Luke?' he says.

'No hurry is there?' Jo says.

'We're eating,' David says.

'Got any to spare?' Jo says.

Marion is about to get her a plate, but David says, 'This is just the two of us, Jo.'

Jo flushes. 'OK,' she says, 'I get the message. Be like that.' And she goes off, slamming the back door.

'What about Luke?' David calls after her, but she's gone.

'He can stay the night,' Marion says. 'At least that way he won't wake us up to be let in.'

'Sorry about Jo,' David says. 'I don't encourage her.'

'I know,' says Marion.

After the curry, Marion puts Luke to bed. She reads him a story from the King Arthur book. She comes down to join David on the sofa. He's watching football and drinking beer.

'Foul!' He shouts so loud that Marion jumps. His mobile rings and, eyes fixed on the TV, he answers it.

'What?' he says. 'OK. OK. See you later.'

'Who was it?' Marion asks, but there's a penalty shoot-out going on and he doesn't answer.

But at half-time he turns the sound down. 'That was Ken,' he says.

'Is he upset?'

'No,' David frowns. 'He rang to

warn us about her.'

'What?'

'He says she's a head case.'

'What?'

'He said, "Watch your back mate, with that one",' David says.

'What does he mean?'

'Search me.'

'She'll make another play for you now,' Marion says.

'Don't worry,' he says. 'She might be playing, but I'm not.'

CHAPTER THIRTEEN

On Sunday afternoon Marion and Luke are in the kitchen, making cookies with funny faces, when Jo comes round.

'Hi Mum,' Luke says.

'I'm going out. Can you mind Luke till later?' Jo says.

'Till when?'

'I'll be back by his bedtime,' Jo

promises.

'Look Mum,' Luke points to one of the cookies, 'this one's you.'

Jo looks. She pulls a face. 'I don't look that bad do I?' she says.

Marion puts the cookies in the oven. 'What's up?' she says. 'Is it Ken?'

'Who?' Jo says.

'What then?'

'He still hasn't told you, has he?'

'What?'

'David. He hasn't told you has he?'

Although it's a hot day Marion shivers. 'Luke, want to go and watch TV?' she says.

'How long will the cookies be?' he says.

'I'll call you when they're ready,' she says. Luke goes through to the other room.

'Told me what?' Marion says when the door is shut.

'He promised he'd tell you,' Jo says.

Marion wants to scream but she

speaks quietly. 'Why don't you tell me?' she says. Her heart is thumping so hard she's sure that Jo can hear it.

'OK,' Jo says. 'But remember, you asked.'

'Go on.'

Marion's hands are shaking. She holds onto the edge of the table to steady herself.

'David is Luke's dad,' Jo says.

'What!'

It's so stupid that Marion almost laughs. It's ridiculous!

'See, I had a fling with him. I fell pregnant.'

'When?'

'His stag party,' Jo says.

Marion takes a deep breath. 'If that was true he would have told me,' she says.

'Would he?' Jo says. 'When I told him I was pregnant he told me to get lost. Actually, he paid me to get lost.'

'David's not like that,' Marion says.

'I'm sick of being a single mum,' Jo

says.

'I don't believe you,' Marion says.

Jo just stands there.

'Even if it was true,' Marion says, 'why would you come back now?'

'I thought I could cope,' Jo says, 'but now I'm broke. And Luke needs his dad. I can't cope on my own any more.'

'I don't believe you,' Marion says.

'Ask him,' Jo says.

'Don't worry. I will,' Marion says. 'Now get out of my house.'

'OK,' Jo says. She smiles. 'I will get David,' she says. 'A boy needs his dad, and look at you—how could anyone fancy you?'

'Get out!' Marion says.

Marion stands in the kitchen with her fists clenched. She looks through the window and sees Jo walk off down the road. She can smell the cookies baking. All those little smiley faces. She goes to see Luke. He's fallen asleep on the sofa. David has dark hair and so does Luke. But lots of people have dark hair. Does Luke look like David?

Marion creeps out and closes the door quietly. She goes into Jo's garden. She knows where the spare key is hidden. She opens the door and goes into Jo's kitchen. It's a mess. Then she goes upstairs. She opens the door to Jo's room and looks round. Jo's clothes are all over the floor. Her lacy knickers and padded bra are lying on a chair. On her dresser there are lipsticks and perfumes and dirty tissues. On the floor by the bed are a pile of magazines and a photo album.

Marion picks up the album and looks inside. There are lots of pictures of Luke from when he was a baby. And there are pictures of David. They've been taken recently. David in the garden, David in the park. And there's a picture of David in a pub. It was taken years ago when he still smoked. He's holding up a beer mug and a cigarette and looking young and drunk. Beside him, with her back to the camera, is a tall redhead. Marion sits on the bed and stares at the picture. She's shivering. She rips the photo out of the album, goes out and locks the door.

When she gets back into her own kitchen she smells the cookies burning. She takes them out of the oven. The chocolate chip eyes have melted and they all look like they're crying.

CHAPTER FOURTEEN

David comes home very pleased with himself. He's been picked as centre-forward for next season. While he's upstairs having a shower, Jo comes round for Luke. Marion doesn't let her in. She calls Luke and he goes home with a plate of burnt cookies. David comes down in a clean shirt with his hair wet. He opens a can of beer.

'What's up?' he says to Marion. 'You look like a wet weekend.'

'Jo came round,' Marion says.

'So?' he says. 'She's always round.'

'You know her from before, don't you?' Marion says.

'No.'

'What's this then?'

Marion shows him the photo.

David takes the photo. He stares at it. 'It's my stag do,' he says.

'You and Jo,' Marion says.

'No,' he says. 'That's not Jo.'

'How can I believe you?' Marion says. She takes a deep breath. 'And she told me that you're Luke's dad,' she says.

'What!' David laughs. He takes a swig of beer. 'My God!' he says. 'She's really losing it. You can't believe her?'

'David.' Marion looks at him. 'Please tell me the truth.'

David looks away. He coughs. Marion starts to shake.

'Was she at your stag do?'

'Truth is, she might have been. A couple of lasses turned up.'

'Why didn't you tell me?'

David shakes his head. 'I didn't recognise her at first.'

Marion stares at him. Suddenly he's a stranger.

Marion's legs go wobbly. She sits down. 'And you slept with her?' she says.

'I was drunk,' he says. 'But no.'

'I don't believe you,' Marion says.

'I promise you I am not Luke's dad. I promise you I never slept with Jo. Come here.' He tries to put his arms round her.

'Get off,' she shouts. She runs up to the bathroom and is sick. She looks at herself in the mirror. She looks awful, pale and fat and old. She goes into the bedroom, takes out her suitcase from under the bed and begins to pack her clothes.

David comes upstairs. 'No,' he says when he sees what she's doing. 'You

71

can't leave.'

Marion doesn't answer. She just throws anything in. She can't think straight. She can't look at him.

'Please,' he says, 'please. This can't be happening.'

Marion takes off her wedding ring and chucks it at him. 'I'm going to my mum's.'

'Don't. Please. Let me prove she's lying,' David says.

'How can I believe anything you say?'

'Don't go,' David says. 'I need you.'

'A boy needs his father,' Marion says. She carries the case down the stairs and out of the door.

She drags it to the car. When she looks back she sees Jo looking out of her window. When Jo sees the suitcase, she waves and gives a great big smile.

CHAPTER FIFTEEN

Marion drives to her mum's with tears in her eyes. She stays there for a week. David rings her at work every day but she won't speak to him. She switches off her mobile. He calls at the house but Marion's mum won't let him see her. He even writes a letter, but Marion doesn't read it. She tears it up and throws it in the bin.

'Maybe you should hear him out,' her mum says. She's always liked David. 'Don't leave him,' she says. 'He's not perfect. But nor is anyone.'

'You're telling *me* he's not perfect!' Marion says.

When she leaves work on Friday, David is standing by her car. In spite of everything, her heart still jumps when she sees him.

'You have to listen,' he says.

'Two minutes,' she says. She folds

her arms and waits.

'No,' he says. 'Come round at 8. There's something you have to see.'

'What?'

'If I can prove that Jo's a liar will you come back?' he says.

'I don't know,' Marion says.

*   *   *

At ten past 8 Marion arrives at the house.

'Quick,' David says. 'Come in. I thought you weren't coming.'

'I nearly didn't.'

'I'm glad you did.' He tries to kiss her but she pulls away.

'What do you want to show me?' she asks.

Tigger jumps into her arms and purrs. She sees that the table is set with a rose in a vase, wine glasses and candles.

'You're not getting round me that easily,' Marion says.

'It's not for you,' David says.

'What?'

'I want you to hide in here,' David says. He opens the tall broom cupboard.

'What?' she says.

'You'll see. Promise not to move until I say so?'

'Why should I promise you anything?'

'It's important,' he says. 'Please. Whatever happens you must not come out until I tell you to. I need to prove something to you. To make you trust me again.'

Marion hesitates, then she shrugs. What's left to lose?

'Quick,' David says. He opens the door and shoves her in, just as Jo comes through the back door with Luke in his pyjamas. The cupboard is too small and the ironing board digs into Marion's back. She crouches down.

'Where's Marion?' Luke asks.

'She's gone,' Jo says. 'Go upstairs to bed.'

'But I want Marion!'

'Get to bed or else,' Jo says.

Luke stamps out of the room and all the way upstairs.

Jo does a twirl for David. 'What do you think?' she says.

She's wearing a new dress, lacy and see through. Her hair is very bright red and so is her lipstick.

'I've been waiting for this day for years,' she says. 'I knew you'd come round in the end.'

'Did you?' David says.

'See,' Jo says, 'you and me is how it's meant to be.'

She puts her arms round David. He looks past her at Marion, through the crack in the door.

'Kiss me then,' Jo says.

'Later,' David says. 'There's no rush is there? Now sit down.'

David pours wine.

'To us,' Jo says.

'To us.' They chink glasses. Marion feels as if she will explode.

'I hope you like ham?' David says.

'I've made a salad.'

Jo sits down and they begin to eat. David keeps looking at his watch. 'OK,' he says, 'now tell me all about it again, how we met, tell me every detail.'

'Why?' Jo says. 'You know as well as I do.'

'I want to hear you say it.'

Jo smiles. Marion can see her cross her legs under the table. She's wearing stockings; Marion sees her bare thighs at the tops.

'I fancied you at school,' Jo says. 'I've loved you since I was 12. But you never noticed me.'

'How could I not notice you?'

'I was different then,' she says. 'I was fat with braces and dark hair.'

David laughs. 'That's cute.'

'No it wasn't. And you were always with someone else.'

'OK.'

'Then you met Marion. And next thing I heard you were getting married. It was a mistake. See, I knew we would end up together. That's how it's meant to be.'

Jo pours herself another glass of wine.

'So that's why me and Karen turned up at your stag do,' Jo says.

'The strippers,' he says.

Jo giggles. 'That was us! God I had to go to the gym every day to get into shape for that.'

'And you've stayed in shape,' David says.

'For you,' she says. 'Marion's let herself go, hasn't she? She must weigh two stone more than me.'

In the cupboard, Marion clenches her fists. She wants to burst out of the door and scratch Jo's eyes out.

'That explains something,' David says. 'No one knew who hired the strippers.'

'No one did,' Jo laughs. 'We just turned up and did it for free.'

'I was very pissed,' David says. He looks at his watch again.

'At last you were looking at me,' Jo

says. She gets up from the table. 'Why don't we go upstairs now and eat later. I could do my strip for you again.'

'Plenty of time,' David says.

'But I want you now.'

The door bell rings.

'Hold it there,' David says. 'I'll just get that.'

Marion watches as Jo puts fresh lipstick on and pours herself a bit more wine. David comes back into the room.

'I've got a surprise for you, Jo,' he says.

A slim blonde comes into the room. 'Hi Jo,' she says.

'Who are you?' Jo says.

'Karen,' David says. 'Don't you remember?'

'Who?' Jo says. 'Remember from when?'

'Are you OK, Jo?' Karen says.

Jo just stares at her.

'David invited me,' Karen says.

'For a reunion,' David says.

'But I don't know you!'

David shakes his head. 'Jo, Jo. Get real, love.'

'I don't remember.' Jo's face is white, she looks confused.

'Jo was just reminding me how you posed as strippers at my stag do,' David says.

'God!' Karen buries her face in her hands for a second. 'That is so embarrassing!'

'This isn't Karen,' Jo says.

'You're really losing it, Jo,' David says. 'But you must have been off your face. Do you really not remember Karen?'

'We were all off our faces,' Karen says. 'I must have been drunk as a skunk to act like that.'

'Remind us exactly what happened, Karen,' David says.

Marion leans forward to hear better and the door opens a bit more but no one notices.

'Well, the plan was for Jo to get off with you. She tried, but you weren't

80

interested.'

'That's how I remember it,' David says, looking over at the cupboard.

'And then she got in a strop and we went off. We went to a club. We both ended up with different men that night. But not you.'

The ironing board falls down with a crash, and Marion crawls out of the cupboard.

'Whoops,' she says. Jo looks so shocked that it makes Marion laugh. She sounds like a mad woman, but she doesn't care.

'Hi Jo,' Marion says. 'Hi Karen.'

'Nice to meet you,' Karen says. 'And then David married Marion, and happy cvcr after,' she finishes.

'Till Jo came along and tried to wreck it,' David adds.

'It's a lie,' Jo says to Marion. 'They're lying. I've never seen her before in my life.'

'See?' David says. 'She'll say anything. No way is Luke my kid,' David says.

'Did she say he was?' Karen says. 'God, Jo!'

'This is a set up,' Jo says. 'He is David's. They're tricking you Marion.'

'Give up, Jo,' David says. 'Get lost.'

Jo stands and looks at him for a moment. 'You know what?' she says. 'I think I will.' And then she lets herself out of the back door and slams it shut.

'She always was a bit—' Karen wiggles her finger at the side of her head.

'A sandwich short of a picnic?'

'A picnic short of a picnic if you ask me!' David says.

David calls Karen a taxi. As she leaves he gives her some money.

'What was that for?' Marion asks.

'Taxi money,' he says. 'Are we OK then?'

'I guess so,' Marion says, but she frowns. It looked like too much money for a taxi fare.

CHAPTER SIXTEEN

In the night Marion hears Luke crying. She gets up to see what is wrong. 'I had a bad dream,' he says. Marion squeezes into bed with Luke and he soon goes back to sleep. She goes back to lie beside David. She listens to him snoring all night but she can't sleep.

Early in the morning she hears a noise outside, but she's too tired to get up and look. She hears Luke go downstairs to watch TV. She goes to sleep then and David wakes her up later with a cup of tea. He gets back into bed.

'Looks like Jo's moving out,' he says. 'There's a van outside. Good riddance.'

'But I won't see Luke again,' Marion says.

'But at least we'll be OK,' David says. 'Thanks for coming back.'

'You're my husband,' Marion says. 'This is my home.'

'And you believe me now? Jo is a lying slag.'

They hear the van drive away. 'I wish Pat had never moved,' Marion says miserably.

'Me too.'

'Jo will be round for Luke in a minute,' Marion says.

'Don't get up,' David says. He tries to kiss her but she pulls away.

'I want to say goodbye to Luke,' she says. 'Stay there. I'll be back.'

'Promise?' David says.

'Promise.' Marion gives him a seductive smile.

'I'm going nowhere,' David says.

When she goes downstairs the TV is on but Luke is asleep on the sofa with Tigger. There is a note on the doormat; it's for David, in Jo's writing. Marion's hands shake as she opens it.

Dear David, it says, I can't cope any more. It's your turn now. Jo.

Marion reads it again and again. She goes to David's jacket and takes out his wallet. A card falls out. Sally Day, Actress, it says. She checks his mobile. There's a text to Sally, telling her to arrive at 8.20 sharp. She puts her head in her hands. Tigger scratches at the door. When she opens it she finds Luke's clothes and toys piled on the doorstep. She sits at the kitchen table and shivers. Luke comes into the kitchen for some breakfast.

'Mum's gone away for a bit,' she says to Luke. She makes him strawberry jam on toast. 'Is that OK?'

'Can I stay with you?' Luke asks.

'Of course you can,' Marion says. 'Maybe we'll go away somewhere shall we? What about Cornwall? We can go to King Arthur's castle.'

'Cool,' Luke says. 'Can we go today?'

'OK,' Marion says. 'You'll have to get dressed quickly.'

She has to think fast. Her suitcase is still at her mum's. She phones for a taxi. She puts Luke's things into carrier bags. She steals all the money from David's wallet and she takes his credit card.

'Hurry up,' David calls from upstairs.

'Won't be long,' Marion says. 'I'm sorting a surprise. Stay there.'

'Can't wait,' he says.

She quietly opens the door and she and Luke stand on the doorstep.

'What about Tigger?' Luke says.

'David can take care of Tigger,' she says. 'And when we're in Cornwall I'll get you a kitten.'

'Promise!' Luke jumps up and down with excitement.

'Shhh,' Marion says. Her hands are sweaty and her heart is beating hard. The taxi has to come before David comes downstairs. She hears him moving about, going into the bathroom.

And then the taxi comes round the

corner.

'Hurry up,' David shouts. 'I'm going off the boil.'

'On my way,' Marion calls. She closes the door quietly and then she and Luke go out into the street and get into the taxi.

'Station please,' says Marion to the driver. As they drive away, Marion sees David standing at the bedroom window. She waves and smiles.